THEN YOU KISSED ME
PRELUDE TO TEQUILA ROSE.

WILLOW WINTERS

Copyright © 2020 by Willow Winters

All rights reserved.

No part of this book may be reproduced in any form or by any electronic or mechanical means, including information storage and retrieval systems, without written permission from the author, except for the use of brief quotations in a book review.

Cover Designer: Lori Jackson Design

ALSO BY WILLOW WINTERS

Small Town Romance

Tequila Rose Book 1
Autumn Night Whiskey Book 2
He tasted like tequila and the fake name I gave him was Rose.
Four years ago, I decided to get over one man, by getting under another. A single night and nothing more.
Now, with a three-year-old in tow, the man I still dream about is staring at me from across the street in the town I grew up in. I don't miss the flash of recognition, or the heat in his gaze.
The chemistry is still there, even after all these years.

I just hope the secrets and regrets don't destroy our second chance before it's even begun.

A Little Bit Dirty

Contemporary Romance Standalones

Knocking Boots (A Novel)

They were never meant to be together.
Charlie is a bartender with noncommittal tendencies.
Grace is looking for the opposite. Commitment. Marriage. A baby.

Promise Me (A Novel)
She gave him her heart. Back when she thought they'd always be together.
Now **Hunter** is home and he wants Violet back.

Tell Me To Stay (A Novella)
He devoured her, and she did the same to him.
Until it all fell apart and Sophie ran as far away from **Madox** as she could.
After all, the two of them were never meant to be together?

Second Chance (A Novella)
No one knows what happened the night that forced them apart. No one can ever know.
But the moment **Nathan** locks his light blue eyes on Harlow again, she is ruined.
She never stood a chance.

Burned Promises (A Novella)
Derek made her a promise. And then he broke it.
That's what happens with your first love.
But Emma didn't expect for Derek to fall back into her life and for her to fall back into his bed.

You Are Mine World

You Are My Reason (You Are Mine Duet book 1)
You Are My Hope (You Are Mine Duet book 2)
Mason and Jules emotionally gripping romantic suspense duet.
One look and Jules was tempted; one taste, addicted.
No one is perfect, but that's how it felt to be in Mason's arms.
But will the sins of his past tear them apart?

You Know I Love You
You Know I Need You

Kat says goodbye to the one man she ever loved even though **Evan** begs her to trust him.
With secrets she couldn't have possibly imagined, Kat is torn between what's right and what was right for them.

Tell Me You Want Me
A sexy office romance with a brooding hero, **Adrian Bradford**, who you can't help but fall head over heels for... in and out of the boardroom.

Valetti Crime Family Series:
A HOT mafia series to sink your teeth into.

Dirty Dom
Becca came to pay off a debt, but **Dominic Valetti** wanted more.
So he did what he's always done, and took what he wanted.

His Hostage
Elle finds herself in the wrong place at the wrong time. The mafia doesn't let witnesses simply walk away.
Regret has a name, and it's **Vincent Valetti**.

Rough Touch
Ava is looking for revenge at any cost so long as she can remember the girl she used to be.
But she doesn't expect **Kane** to show up and show her kindness that will break her.

Cuffed Kiss
Tommy Valetti is a thug, a mistake, and everything Tonya needs; the answers to numb the pain of her past.

Bad Boy
Anthony is the hitman for the Valetti familia, and damn good at what he does. They want men to talk, he makes them talk. They want men gone, bang - it's done. It's as simple as that.
Until Catherine.

Those Boys Are Trouble (Valetti Crime Family Collection)

To Be Claimed Saga
A hot tempting series of fated love, lust-filled secrets and the beginnings of an epic war.

Wounded Kiss

Gentle Scars

Read Willow's sexiest and most talked about romances in the Merciless World

This Love Hurts Trilogy
This Love Hurts
But I Need You
And I Love You the Most

An epic tale of both betrayal and all-consuming love...
Marcus, the villain.
Cody Walsh, the FBI agent who knows too much.
And Delilah, the lawyer caught in between.

What I Would do for You (This Love Hurts Trilogy Collection)

A Kiss to Tell (a standalone novel)
They lived on the same street and went to the same school, although he was a year ahead. Even so close, he was untouchable.
Sebastian was bad news and Chloe was the sad girl who didn't belong.
Then one night changed everything.

Possessive (a standalone novel)
It was never love with **Daniel Cross** and she never thought it would be. It was only lust from a distance. Unrequited love maybe.
He's a man Addison could never have, for so many reasons.

Merciless Saga
Merciless
Heartless
Breathless
Endless

Ruthless, crime family leader **Carter Cross** should've known Aria would ruin him the moment he saw her. Given to Carter to start a war; he was too eager to accept. But what he didn't know was what Aria would do to him. He didn't know that she would change everything.

All He'll Ever Be (Merciless Series Collection of all 4 novels)

Irresistible Attraction Trilogy
A Single Glance
A Single Kiss

A Single Touch

Bethany is looking for answers and to find them she needs one of the brothers of an infamous crime family, **Jase Cross**.
Even a sizzling love affair won't stop her from getting what she needs.
But Bethany soon comes to realise Jase will be her downfall, and she's determined to be his just the same.

Irresistible Attraction (A Single Glance Trilogy Collection)

Hard to Love Series
Hard to Love
Desperate to Touch
Tempted to Kiss
Easy to Fall

Eight years ago she ran from him.
Laura should have known he'd come for her. Men like **Seth King** always get what they want.
Laura knows what Seth wants from her, and she knows it comes with a steep price.
However it's a risk both of them will take.

Not My Heart to Break (Hard to Love Series Collection)

Tease Me Once
Tease me once... I'll kiss you twice.
Declan Cross' story from the Merciless World.

Spin off of the Merciless World

Love the Way Series
Kiss Me
Hold Me
Love Me

With everything I've been through, and the unfortunate way we met, the last thing I thought I'd be focused on is the fact that I love the way you kiss me.

Extended epilogues to the Merciless World Novels
A Kiss To Keep (more of Sebastian and Chloe)
Seductive (more of Daniel and Addison)
Effortless (more of Carter and Aria)
Never to End (more of Seth and Laura)

Sexy, thrilling with a touch of dark Standalone Novels

Broken (Standalone)

Kade is ruthless and cold hearted in the criminal world.

They gave Olivia to him. To break. To do as he'd like. All because she was in the wrong place at the wrong time. But there are secrets that change everything. And once he has her, he's never letting her go.

Forget Me Not (Standalone novel)

She loved a boy a long time ago. He helped her escape and she left him behind. Regret followed her every day after.

Jay, the boy she used to know, came back, a man. With a grip strong enough to keep her close and a look in his eyes that warned her to never dare leave him again.

It's dark and twisted.

But that doesn't make it any less of what it is.

A love story. Our love story.

It's Our Secret (Standalone novel)

It was only a little lie. That's how stories like these get started.

But with every lie Allison tells, **Dean** sees through it. She didn't know what would happen. But with all the secrets and lies, she never thought she'd fall for him.

Collections of shorts and novellas

Don't Let Go
A collection of stories including:
Infatuation
Desires in the Night and Keeping Secrets
Bad Boy Next Door

Kisses and Wishes
A collection of holiday stories including:
One Holiday Wish
Collared for Christmas
Stolen Mistletoe Kisses

All I Want is a Kiss (A Holiday short)
Olivia thought fleeting weekends would be enough and it always was, until the distance threatened to tear her and **Nicholas** apart for good.

Highest Bidder Series:

Bought
Sold
Owned
Given

From USA Today best selling authors, Willow Winters and Lauren Landish, comes a sexy and forbidden series of standalone romances.

Highest Bidder Collection (All four Highest Bidder Novels)

Bad Boy Standalones, cowritten with Lauren Landish:

Inked
Tempted
Mr. CEO

Three novels featuring sexy powerful heroes. Three romances that are just as swoon-worthy as they are tempting.

Simply Irresistible (A Bad Boy Collection)

Forsaken, (A Dark Romance cowritten with B. B. Hamel)

Grace is stolen and gifted to him; Geo a dominating, brutal and a cold hearted killer.
However, with each gentle touch and act of kindness that lures her closer to him, Grace is finding it impossible to remember why she should fight him.

View Willow's entire collection and full reading order at willowwinterswrites.com/reading-order

Happy reading and best wishes,
Willow xx

THEN YOU KISSED ME

By Willow Winters

I thought I had life all figured out… and then you kissed me.

Then You Kissed Me is a prelude to Tequila Rose.

BRODY

I'm not supposed to be here, in this bar, to flirt with a girl I don't even know... it's all I can think when I notice her.

Her curves are not why I'm here, although they're exactly why I'm standing in the middle of the bar, stopped in my tracks before I can even sit down. *She's* not on my to-do list tonight.

Even with the internal voice scolding every thought I have, I know the second I lay eyes on her, perched on a stool with a faraway look in her striking hazel eyes, that there's something about this girl that makes it harder to keep walking than it should be.

"You can seat yourself," a hostess, with a tight but kind smile and three tall menus for the Blue Room wrapped in stamped black leather, tells me as she walks past at the pace of a woman who's busy as all hell in this crowded bar. "Thanks," I answer the back of her white dress as she heads off.

This place is made to look like a modern day speakeasy with the clean décor but darkened corners. And packed at that. Makes sense, I guess, since it's a college town. It's amazing there's even a seat open at the bar. Especially one next to a woman like the one in that tight red dress.

My good friend Griffin told me about this bar. He said it was a good place to think since it's always busy and the chatter and ambiance makes for decent white noise. He knows the shit I'm going through and a beer and good atmosphere will do wonders to take your mind off things you'd rather not deal with. Well according to him.

Taking a glance at the far end of the bar that separates the large space into two halves, I'm sure Griffin didn't have that blonde at the bar in mind when he said I should go clear my head. Sit down. Have a beer. Watch the game. Those were my marching orders.

Getting lost in her is exactly what I'd rather do than spend the night drinking alone, waiting on Griffin to be done his ... whatever the hell he had to do. Of all the people in here, she's the only one I really notice. Although it's obvious she did that by design.

She's alone at the bar, even though her short, red dress is a show piece. The way the silky fabric rides up her thigh and she blushes when she notices… it does something to me. The mix of sultry and innocence. Like she's not sure how much she should give away. She's not used to doing this. This young girl on the hunt for a good time charade.

If nothing else, I know if I don't sit next to her, someone else will. If I don't take her home tonight some other asshole in this place damn sure will. The moment that realization hits me, I know there's no way in hell I'm going to let that happen.

Smirking, I watch her throw back the pink cocktail and make my way to her as she watches the crowd. I'm no knight in shining armor, but I know how to buy a girl a drink.

I've decided, after less than a minute of watching her, that she's on the prowl, but too damn cute and innocent to know what she's doing. Telling myself that's all this is, I drag out the bar stool and ask her if she needs another drink.

Her eyes hit me first then the blush in her cheeks rises all the way up to her temple. My blood simmers and travels lower. I was right, she's a shy little thing to be sitting alone, wearing a dress that's meant for a good time.

She keeps looking at me, her fingers fiddling with the rim of her empty glass. Even that small movement is sexy as hell. The smile is sweet and the fact that she's too busy eying me up to realize she hasn't answered makes me laugh.

That gruff sound that comes deep from my chest turns her cheeks to an even hotter shade of red. I might be man candy to some girls, but damn she doesn't hide it at all.

"Yes please, if you're offering," she finally answers, twirling the ends of her wavy hair around the tips of her fingers flirtatiously. Her voice is soft, and gentle, but with a playfulness that's undeniable. And her lips… fuck, my cock is already hardening.

Better than that, she can barely keep her gaze on me without smiling even harder.

She's fucking adorable. The perfect mix of sweet and sexy. Just knowing I get to her makes the black tee shirt that's already tight on my broad shoulders even tighter. I know I look blue collar; I can't hide that rough side of me. Dark jeans and a black tee shirt are about as dressed up as I ever get.

This girl looks like anything but that.

But the way she fidgets and keeps glancing at me like I'm man candy she hasn't tasted, lets me know she's as interested in me as I am in her.

Thank fuck. I'm not from around here, never went to college, and it's been a while since I've dated anyone.

She's not eye fucking me, she's eye glancing me because she's too bashful to outright stare at me. Everything about her makes me smile. She's too damn cute to be here alone.

Small talk is easy with her. This girl named Rose. It suits her with the red dress and delicate features of her slender neck. Throughout the night, all I can think about is kissing her there. Every time her hand slips down to my thigh. Playful and seemingly innocent but I know she knows what she's doing.

Every hour that passes, the place empties out more and more. She doesn't seem to notice or care. She's too busy asking me questions that are far too sweet and demure to elicit anything more than a laugh and more of those stolen touches. *What's my favorite color? What's my best friend's name? What's a joke I'd never tell my parents?*

Until she asks what brought me here since I'm not in college. Saying I came to visit a friend worked the first time, but she pries deeper so I hit her back with the same kind of question. The kind of question where there's a piece of it you don't want to exist.

"What brought you here tonight? In a red dress, sitting all alone?"

BRODY

*H*er slender fingers slip on the straw in her glass of water and her gaze drops to the bar. At first, I think she's not going to answer, but she surprises me. Her bottom lip slips out from her teeth, grabbing all my attention to her kissable lips before Rose answers me, "I wanted to meet someone tonight."

"Is that right?"

"Yeah," she nods, the tension that was there for a split second when I asked her the question vanishes and her small hand lands on my thigh again, doing all sorts of things to me that the simplest of touches shouldn't be capable of doing. Thump, thump, my blood pumps harder as she brings her lips to the shell of my ear.

"I kind of want to go home with you tonight," her warm breath sends a shiver down my neck, past my shoulders and doesn't stop.

"You're tipsy," it's only a comment, but there's an invitation hidden in my tone. I give her the way out though, just in case it's only liquid courage. "I could take you home, drop you off if you want?"

"You're cute," Rose whispers around her drink as she peeks up at me with her thick lashes. My grin is easy. All of tonight has been easy. I haven't thought about a damn thing except what she has to say. When the lights turn on behind the bar, the music turns off and the check hits the table, I slap the cash down, tipping the bartender well.

I ask this sweet Rose as she climbs off the stool, standing next to me a head shorter and her gaze focused on the dip in my throat, "What do you want to do?"

She sets her finger right where she's looking, her touch gentle and her voice nearly lost in the air between us, "I want to kiss you right here."

That does it. Wrapping an arm around her waist, I pull her in close and revel in the feel of her soft body against mine as her heels hit the floor and she squeals in delight.

She doesn't let go of me, and in the cab she

fucking tortures me, kissing me just below my ear on that tender spot I thought about kissing her.

"Not yet, my wild Rose," I half scold her in a whisper but as she pulls away, I capture her lips in mine. The kiss is searing, that first one in the back of the cab, with the taste of temptation and tequila mixing. My blood runs hot, my fingers inching up her thigh the way she did it to me all night. The only difference is I'm touching bare skin and the light, tender touch isn't enough.

Her gasp fills the cab when I pull away and when the cab driver looks back at us in the rearview, I keep my gaze forward, as if nothing at all is going on back here against his black leather seat.

As if I don't want to rip off her dress and push my hand between her legs, and rock my palm against her clit.

"You're already hard," her whisper comes with a hint of awe as she grips me through my jeans. Fuck, my head falls back and I close my eyes when the cab driver tries to meet my gaze again, his eyebrows much higher up on his forehead.

"Wait just five more minutes, Rose."

"I don't want to wait." Her protest is adorable, but there's no way this driver is getting a show.

"You're killing me," I groan and decide I should

satisfy her before I come undone and take her right here.

With my fingers spearing through her gorgeous blonde locks, I mold my lips against hers, stealing her surprise gasp and loving the soft moan of pleasure she gives me when I kiss her again. Her fingers play along the back of my neck, her tongue dancing with mine and I make sure to keep my hands right where they are on the small of her waist. One move, and I swear I won't be able to stop.

I've never been so relieved to hear a cab driver tell me "we're here" and hand over the cash.

Rose's cheeks are a gorgeous hue of pink that travels down to her chest.

Griffin's not here when I unlock the apartment door. She's in my arms, her legs wrapped around my waist, her ankles hooked behind me with her heels digging into my ass before I can even kick the door shut behind me.

This girl knows what she wants and I've never been so eager to give it to her, to satisfy every sordid thought I know she had back at the bar.

I don't bother turning on the lights to Griffin's bachelor apartment, barren of everything that makes a home a home considering his student budget.

She doesn't need to see any of this place, she

doesn't want to either. All she wants is to get in bed and as I kick my shoes off, our lips still locked in place, I'm just fine with that.

Her ass fits perfectly in my palms, but this damn dress is in the way.

My desire to shred it is only tamed by the fact that I know this is all she has to wear when this is over and I sure as shit know Griffin doesn't have any chick's clothes here.

When I toss her on the bed, the faded light shining through the slits in the blinds and casting the most beautiful shadows along the curves of her neck and breasts, she takes in a deep inhale, arching her back like she's been deprived of breath all the while.

That's when I realize the heavy rising and falling of my own chest, and sharp need to be buried inside of her that overrides any other sane thought that might come to me.

My jeans are off, my shirt ripped over my head and tossed carelessly on the floor in seconds. Her dress and lace underwear are quick to join my pile of clothes.

"I love the way your hands feel," she moans as I cup her breast in my hand. Her chest is small but full and when I run the pad my thumb over her hardened peaks, her head falls back, her lips part just slightly and her eyes close. I let her lose herself in the pleasure I give her, skimming my hands over her body, kissing every inch of her until I find her hot and glistening between her thighs.

With my breathing finally calm again, and hers ragged as she lays under me, I pump my cock once in my hand to get her attention. Her eyes go wide and that seems to wake her up.

She doesn't say anything, but her gaze doesn't leave my length and she stills on the bed.

Fuck. That is not a good sign.

"You alright?" I ask her realizing something is very fucking wrong right now. Please don't back out. Please, for the love of all things holy, I need to be inside this woman more than I need to breathe.

Licking her lower lip, her body relaxes only slightly when she looks up at me and says, "You're… you're really big." I don't break her hazel stare.

"I'll go slow."

She nods and gets settled, the sheets rustling as she lays down, far more aware than I think she's been all night.

Nestling my hips between her thighs, she spreads her legs wider for me. The first kiss I give her is in the crook of her neck, that spot I was dying to kiss before. With the head of my dick pressing against her warmth, I let the tip of my nose run up her neck and take my time kissing her again.

The warmth comes back to her body, every small touch bringing her closer and closer to the edge of writhing under me. I nip her lower lip and she kisses me desperately.

That's my cue to enter her in a swift but slow, deep stroke. I stare down at her as I push all of myself into her. Her nails dig into my back, her reddened lips, swollen from kissing me, making a beautiful little "o".

And her gaze stays on mine as her heart pounds in time with mine. I stay that way, letting her stretch and get adjusted until she finally breathes again. It takes longer than I thought it would, but every second is worth it.

The next stroke is faster, deeper and then harder. Working my way up to taking her like I want. The slapping sound due to her arousal and my pistoning hips stirs with her strangled moans of pleasure. She tilts her hips every time she comes and it lets me in deeper as her pussy flutters around my cock.

I want to come more times than I can count, but I can't get enough of the feeling when she gets off. The sound of her crying out my name. The pleas she makes not to stop. Every little thing she does is mesmerizing.

When I finally have my release, it's four o clock in the morning and her breathing comes in chaotic pants, her body well spent and well fucked.

"Can I crash here?" her voice is a whispered wish, sleeping dragging her down deeper into the covers. As if I'd kick her out. *What kind of men is she used to?*

"Yeah, of course," I answer her, pulling the covers around us both. I'm rewarded with a small smile on her gorgeous face and a hum of satisfaction as she scoots closer to me. Apparently, she's a cuddler. A piece of me is more than satisfied with that side of her and the feel of her against me and the easy way she lets me hold her.

Her body molds to mine, her soft curves not leaving an inch of space between us in the bed. The bed protests with a groan at every small movement we make. The dim light that slips through the blinds, provided only by the street lights, lays against her soft skin, and begs me to kiss her again. Right there in the crook of her neck, just to see if she'll shiver again at my touch. If it wasn't for her steady breathing and the angelic look on her face as she sleeps, I'd wake her again and take her again. There's something about her that's addictive. Something that calls to a deeper side of me, telling me she needs it just as much as I do.

Lying beside the messy halo of her blonde locks, with the floral and fragrant, I drift off. Sleeping beside her lures me to sweet dreams of her soft moans as I take her again and again; I sleep better than I have in months.

BRODY

I'm not prepared to wake up alone. Finding her side of the bed long gone and cold is a bit of a surprise to say the least. I want her again. I dreamed of the sounds she'd make early in the morning. Her legs wrapped around my waist as I pounded into her. Fuck, I can't wait to hear her cry out as her nails scraped down my back. There's no better way to start a morning than a good hard fuck. But the house is empty.

She didn't even leave me a note, my wild Rose.

That realization makes me laugh as I shake my head and pour myself a cup of coffee. She must've left before the sun was even up. I remember her asking if she could stay last night and I wonder if she's been kicked out before and didn't want to go through that again.

That's the first sign of unease I feel, but I shake it off, feeling confident that I'll see her again at the bar tonight.

It was a wild night and missing her only makes me want her more. Just like the red dress at the bar, she knew what she was doing. Playing hard to get.

I thought she was toying with me. I was so damn certain I'd see her again.

I only went to that bar to look for her. I only stayed in that town an extra week, waiting for her. Every day that passed, the disappointment grew deeper. I decided one day we'd meet again, and I'd make her ass pay for not saying good bye. I got a lot wrong in my life, but I've never been so grateful that I was right about running into Rose again. Even if it was four years later, in another town.

Even if she'd kept something from me that changed everything.

I thought I had life all figured out… and then she kissed me.

TEQUILA ROSE

He tasted like tequila and the fake name I gave him was Rose.

Four years ago, I decided to get over one man, by getting under another. A single night and nothing more.

I found my handsome stranger with a shot glass and charming but devilish smile at the end of the bar. The desire that hit his eyes the second they landed on me ignited a spark inside me, instant and hot. He was perfect and everything I didn't know I needed. That one night may have ended, but I left with much more than a memory.

Four years later, and with a three-year-old in tow, the man I still dream about is staring at me from across the street in the town I grew up in. I don't miss the flash of recognition, or the heat in his gaze.

The chemistry is still there, even after all these years.

I just hope the secrets and regrets don't destroy our second chance before it's even begun.

Don't stop reading! Find out what happened next! Get your copy of Tequila Rose now!

Want a signed copy of Then You Kissed Me or any of my other books? Shop now at www.willowwinterswrites.com/shop and use **ebook20 to save** 20%. Coupon also works on bookish merch in my shop. Happy shopping xoxo

Follow me on BOOKBUB to be the first to know about my sales!

Sign up for Text Alerts:
US residents: Text WILLOW to 797979
UK residents: Text WWINTERS to 82228

And if you're on Facebook, join my reader group, Willow Winters' Wildflowers for special updates and lots of fun!

ALSO BY WILLOW WINTERS

Small Town Romance

Tequila Rose Book 1
Autumn Night Whiskey Book 2
He tasted like tequila and the fake name I gave him was Rose.
Four years ago, I decided to get over one man, by getting under another. A single night and nothing more.
Now, with a three-year-old in tow, the man I still dream about is staring at me from across the street in the town I grew up in. I don't miss the flash of recognition, or the heat in his gaze.
The chemistry is still there, even after all these years.

I just hope the secrets and regrets don't destroy our second chance before it's even begun.

A Little Bit Dirty

Contemporary Romance Standalones

Knocking Boots (A Novel)

They were never meant to be together.
Charlie is a bartender with noncommittal tendencies.
Grace is looking for the opposite. Commitment. Marriage. A baby.

Promise Me (A Novel)

She gave him her heart. Back when she thought they'd always be together.
Now **Hunter** is home and he wants Violet back.

Tell Me To Stay (A Novella)

He devoured her, and she did the same to him.
Until it all fell apart and Sophie ran as far away from **Madox** as she could.
After all, the two of them were never meant to be together?

Second Chance (A Novella)

No one knows what happened the night that forced them apart. No one can ever know.
But the moment **Nathan** locks his light blue eyes on Harlow again, she is ruined.
She never stood a chance.

Burned Promises (A Novella)

Derek made her a promise. And then he broke it.
That's what happens with your first love.
But Emma didn't expect for Derek to fall back into her life and for her to fall back into his bed.

You Are Mine World

You Are My Reason (You Are Mine Duet book 1)
You Are My Hope (You Are Mine Duet book 2)
Mason and Jules emotionally gripping romantic suspense duet.
One look and Jules was tempted; one taste, addicted.
No one is perfect, but that's how it felt to be in Mason's arms.
But will the sins of his past tear them apart?

You Know I Love You
You Know I Need You

ALSO BY WILLOW WINTERS

Kat says goodbye to the one man she ever loved even though **Evan** begs her to trust him.
With secrets she couldn't have possibly imagined, Kat is torn between what's right and what was right for them.

Tell Me You Want Me
A sexy office romance with a brooding hero, **Adrian Bradford**, who you can't help but fall head over heels for... in and out of the boardroom.

Valetti Crime Family Series:
A HOT mafia series to sink your teeth into.

Dirty Dom
Becca came to pay off a debt, but **Dominic Valetti** wanted more.
So he did what he's always done, and took what he wanted.

His Hostage
Elle finds herself in the wrong place at the wrong time. The mafia doesn't let witnesses simply walk away.
Regret has a name, and it's **Vincent Valetti**.

Rough Touch

Ava is looking for revenge at any cost so long as she can remember the girl she used to be.

But she doesn't expect **Kane** to show up and show her kindness that will break her.

Cuffed Kiss

Tommy Valetti is a thug, a mistake, and everything Tonya needs; the answers to numb the pain of her past.

Bad Boy

Anthony is the hitman for the Valetti familia, and damn good at what he does. They want men to talk, he makes them talk. They want men gone, bang - it's done. It's as simple as that.

Until Catherine.

Those Boys Are Trouble (Valetti Crime Family Collection)

To Be Claimed Saga

A hot tempting series of fated love, lust-filled secrets and the beginnings of an epic war.

Wounded Kiss

ALSO BY WILLOW WINTERS

Gentle Scars

Read Willow's sexiest and most talked about romances in the Merciless World

This Love Hurts Trilogy
This Love Hurts
But I Need You
And I Love You the Most

An epic tale of both betrayal and all-consuming love...
Marcus, the villain.
Cody Walsh, the FBI agent who knows too much.
And Delilah, the lawyer caught in between.

What I Would do for You (This Love Hurts Trilogy Collection)

A Kiss to Tell (a standalone novel)
They lived on the same street and went to the same school, although he was a year ahead. Even so close, he was untouchable.
Sebastian was bad news and Chloe was the sad girl who didn't belong.
Then one night changed everything.

Possessive (a standalone novel)
It was never love with **Daniel Cross** and she never thought it would be. It was only lust from a distance. Unrequited love maybe.
He's a man Addison could never have, for so many reasons.

Merciless Saga
Merciless
Heartless
Breathless
Endless

Ruthless, crime family leader **Carter Cross** should've known Aria would ruin him the moment he saw her. Given to Carter to start a war; he was too eager to accept. But what he didn't know was what Aria would do to him. He didn't know that she would change everything.

All He'll Ever Be (Merciless Series Collection of all 4 novels)

Irresistible Attraction Trilogy
A Single Glance
A Single Kiss

ALSO BY WILLOW WINTERS

A Single Touch

Bethany is looking for answers and to find them she needs one of the brothers of an infamous crime family, **Jase Cross**.
Even a sizzling love affair won't stop her from getting what she needs.
But Bethany soon comes to realise Jase will be her downfall, and she's determined to be his just the same.

Irresistible Attraction (A Single Glance Trilogy Collection)

Hard to Love Series
Hard to Love
Desperate to Touch
Tempted to Kiss
Easy to Fall

Eight years ago she ran from him.
Laura should have known he'd come for her. Men like **Seth King** always get what they want.
Laura knows what Seth wants from her, and she knows it comes with a steep price.
However it's a risk both of them will take.

ALSO BY WILLOW WINTERS

Not My Heart to Break (Hard to Love Series Collection)

Tease Me Once
Tease me once... I'll kiss you twice.
Declan Cross' story from the Merciless World.

Spin off of the Merciless World

Love the Way Series
Kiss Me
Hold Me
Love Me

With everything I've been through, and the unfortunate way we met, the last thing I thought I'd be focused on is the fact that I love the way you kiss me.

Extended epilogues to the Merciless World Novels
A Kiss To Keep (more of Sebastian and Chloe)
Seductive (more of Daniel and Addison)
Effortless (more of Carter and Aria)
Never to End (more of Seth and Laura)

ALSO BY WILLOW WINTERS

Sexy, thrilling with a touch of dark Standalone Novels

Broken (Standalone)

Kade is ruthless and cold hearted in the criminal world.

They gave Olivia to him. To break. To do as he'd like. All because she was in the wrong place at the wrong time. But there are secrets that change everything. And once he has her, he's never letting her go.

Forget Me Not (Standalone novel)

She loved a boy a long time ago. He helped her escape and she left him behind. Regret followed her every day after.

Jay, the boy she used to know, came back, a man. With a grip strong enough to keep her close and a look in his eyes that warned her to never dare leave him again.

It's dark and twisted.

But that doesn't make it any less of what it is.

A love story. Our love story.

It's Our Secret (Standalone novel)

It was only a little lie. That's how stories like these get started.

But with every lie Allison tells, **Dean** sees through it. She didn't know what would happen. But with all the secrets and lies, she never thought she'd fall for him.

Collections of shorts and novellas

Don't Let Go
A collection of stories including:
Infatuation
Desires in the Night and Keeping Secrets
Bad Boy Next Door

Kisses and Wishes
A collection of holiday stories including:
One Holiday Wish
Collared for Christmas
Stolen Mistletoe Kisses

All I Want is a Kiss (A Holiday short)
Olivia thought fleeting weekends would be enough and it always was, until the distance threatened to tear her and **Nicholas** apart for good.

Highest Bidder Series:

ALSO BY WILLOW WINTERS

Bought
Sold
Owned
Given

From USA Today best selling authors, Willow Winters and Lauren Landish, comes a sexy and forbidden series of standalone romances.

Highest Bidder Collection (All four Highest Bidder Novels)

Bad Boy Standalones, cowritten with Lauren Landish:

Inked
Tempted
Mr. CEO

Three novels featuring sexy powerful heroes. Three romances that are just as swoon-worthy as they are tempting.

Simply Irresistible (A Bad Boy Collection)

Forsaken, (A Dark Romance cowritten with B. B. Hamel)

ALSO BY WILLOW WINTERS

Grace is stolen and gifted to him; Geo a dominating, brutal and a cold hearted killer.
However, with each gentle touch and act of kindness that lures her closer to him, Grace is finding it impossible to remember why she should fight him.

View Willow's entire collection and full reading order at willowwinterswrites.com/reading-order

Happy reading and best wishes,
Willow xx

ABOUT WILLOW WINTERS

Thank you so much for reading my romances. I'm just a stay at home mom and avid reader turned author and I couldn't be happier.
I hope you love my books as much as I do!

More by W Winters
www.willowwinterswrites.com/books/

Sign up for my Newsletter to get all my romance releases, sales, sneak peeks and a **FREE** Romance, **Burned Promises**

If you prefer *text alerts* so you don't miss any of my new releases, text
US residents: Text WILLOW to 797979

UK residents: Text WWINTERS to 82228

Contact W Winters
Bookbub | Twitter | Goodreads | Tiktok
Instagram | Facebook Page | Website

Check out Willow Winters Wildflowers on Facebook - If I'm not writing, I'm in one of these groups!

Made in the USA
Middletown, DE
11 July 2024